B.

MW01172828

BRUDDER
FALL
ME
DOWN

LUCY LEDORA PARKER

BRUDDER FALL ME DOWN

Published by Sistahs With Ink Foundation

Edited by Passion D. N. Rutledge

Book Cover design by: Dynasty's Visionary Design Publication

Special Tribute page designed by BeNaiah Williams

Interior Book Designer: Luella Hill-Dudley

ISBN: 9798483365457

Library of Congress Control Number: 2021919861

Copyright © 2021 Lucy Ledora Parker

Dedication

First and foremost, I would like to give honor and thanks to God for allowing me space on this Earth, for giving me the ability to tell my story, and for making my dream come true.

I would also like to dedicate this book, my dream come true, to several family members and friends for their constant support and encouragement throughout this 40-year process:

Special thank you to: Timira Ray' Shawn Ledora Gilmer, Aaron Loyd Ray Gilmer Sr., Ella Mae McQuater, Mary Madsen, Vickie Bloodworth, Tiffany Chatman, Rachel Jones, Antionette Gillis & "Big Daddy", Barbara & David Alee, First Lady Linda and Bishop Norris Cooley, and Vanette Davenport .

May God forever wrap His arm around you make your dreams come true.

Acknowledgements

Now as I look around and think things over, I think of that one friend that has been with me for so many years. After 60 years together, she has become my sister, confidant, and prayer partner. I know she will laugh as she reads this autobiography. I pray she will know that this is my highest form of praise to another mere mortal. I pray that every two little girls find a way to turn Kindergarten into old age and a lifetime of friendship. Margaret Lewis Fowler is Gail to my Oprah.

"Write the book, write the book…write the damn book!" she would say to me.

During our many years together, she has screamed, hollered, and pushed. Then, finally, after sixty years of believing and never losing faith, she put her foot down. She helped me grab hold of that monster called courage and put it all on paper—hence this project. I thank her for her friendship.

To Margaret Fowler, thank you for never giving up on me, although, there had to be days of doubt; for never leaving me although it seemed I was procrastinating, but, as you know, I have learned to trust in Jesus; and I will always trust in you my "Sistah".

Special acknowledgement and thanks to my sister Luella Hill-Dudley, CEO and Founder of Sistah's With Ink. She is the "ear" that heard the voice of God tell her to have my story published and make my lifelong dream a reality. I could never thank you enough dear sister. If one soul comes to Christ because of these words, there will be a star in your heavenly crown.

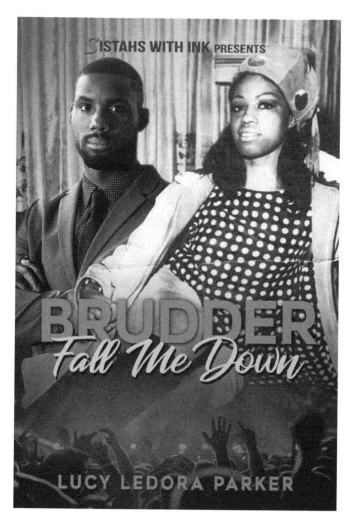

AUTOBIOGRAPHY OF A SPIRITUAL JOURNEY

Table of Contents

TRIBUTE

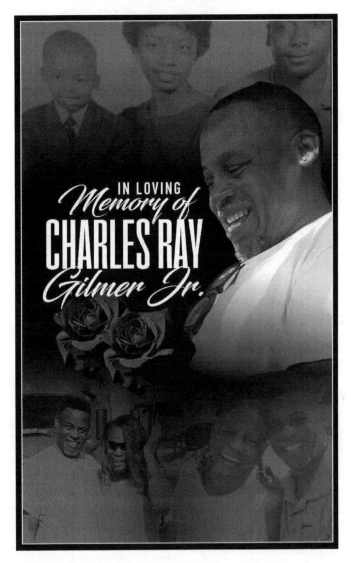

PREFACE

It has taken me thirty years to write this autobiography. Why now, you may ask? Because it is time. Why not thirty years ago? My fear of failure. Fear of the people in my life discovering the deep, dark secret that has paralyzed me all these many years.

A few years back, I sat on my sofa reading an article in a famous women's magazine. An actress was being interviewed concerning a new role she was playing—the role of an addict. Her response to one particular question simply bowled me over. It felt like she spoke directly to me.

"Substance abuse is not an individual's job in life, and is not a definition of who they are," she had said.

My years of substance abuse have not been without the customary fakes, phonies, and wild nights. I have dated high-rollers and then partied big time in some big-time places with many big-time people. I have been flown from one end of this world to the other and gone on countless cruises. Once, I traveled by charter plane to San Francisco just for a football game then hopped in a helicopter at half-time to go to another game in Oakland. I lived the life of dreams. But it was all a façade.

Addressing this very topic—substance abuse— inspired me to write this book. I struggled with an addiction to cocaine for forty years. Now that may seem like a lifetime, but day in and day out, special occasions, parties, and travels add up over time. There were spaces of time in between when I did not do drugs. But for the most part, cocaine played a huge part in my life.

There is such a stigma attached to this and any other drug addiction. People steal, cheat, kill, and yes even sell their babies because of it. I've never actually met anyone that sold their children but I'm sure along the way there were times when I neglected mine. Because of the stigma, I gave up on the things that had once meant so much to me. Where church had once played a positive role in my life I stopped going. Where I used to visit old friends and family for that connection, I stopped visiting. I came to a point where I desired to hide from everyone. All the while, in the back of my mind, I prayed to God that if He delivered me from the hands of cocaine and cigarettes I would write this book in His honor. This is my story.

Chapter I
My Beloved Family

I was born in Madison County, Mississippi, on a cold January morning: my mother was home alone when her labor started. It has been told to me that there was no one nearby to help her or to go for any help. I don't know where my other sisters were at the time or whether they even lived in the same place with my mother.

I've also been told I looked like a piece of liver with hair when I burst from my mother's womb. I weighed less than a pound and my eyes were wide open; that was rare for those times. When I later met my mother and we conversed, she told me I laid there between her legs looking up at her as she faded in and out from the shock. I would sneeze and that is all that kept her from falling into complete unconsciousness. She confessed she felt terrified but my little look gave her hope.

Some hours after my birth, my grandfather stopped by my mother's house and found us. One month later, they placed me in the hands of my 12-year-old cousin, Jessie James Robinson, and took me to live with his mother—my aunt Lela Hopkins. I had a secure life with my aunt Lela and her husband Guy for 19 years. That is who I call family.

Aunt Lela told me my responsibility was to pay my keep. By the time I was five, she had taught me how to cut, boil, and fry salted pork; cook rice to perfection with every grain standing along; kill chickens by wringing their necks; and bake cornbread that all our neighbors admired. I also washed, ironed, and took care of the livestock.

found and sanitized her douche bag; and shoved her hemorrhoids back in her ass when they fell out. She would work me so hard that by the time I finally got to bed, it would be time to get up again before I could even wind my body down to sleep.

My days often began at three in the morning. Guy worked as a plumber and he had to be at work very early in the mornings. Plus, Aunt Lela was always sick. She had great stomach pains that always started in the middle of the night. She would come into my room, shake me awake, and tell me to call Dr. Williams. Night after night, year after year, we went through this ritual. The doctor seemed unable to help her, so it became my duty to stay awake— walking with her and rubbing her stomach to ease the pain until she felt better. Only then could I sleep. an hour here, twenty minutes there, but never a full eight hours.

Miss Lela is what I called her on the days we were friends. Other days she allowed me to call her "grandmamma" even though she wasn't my grandmother. I had an older sister, Sua; we were 18 months apart. So, it came as no real surprise when in 1941 I overheard my mother begging her sister, Lela, to also take in my sister. All so that my mother could go off to California with her new husband and baby boy. Lela told mama "no" in no uncertain terms. Despite that, mama put a mattress on top of her new husband's Packard, drove to Lela's, and left my older sister and the mattress on the sidewalk in front of Lela's house. Sua made the mistake of calling Lela "mama" one day.

"I am not your mother, so call me by another name," Lela quickly told Sua.

"I will call you grandmamma," Sua replied, and the name stuck.

My grandfather, Henry Parker, of Apache Indian and African descent, often went by his Indian name: White Head Daddy. Henry Parker was already a married man and a father of eight when he met my maternal grandmother—a 16-year-old Irish girl. Lela told me my grandmother came to America with her brother Andrew. I still don't know much about her but Lela sounded very serious when she told me about her day after day. She did this daily to make me aware of and proud of my Irish bloodline. Lela attempted to drive the Irish bloodline into my soul. She was very unhappy with the black bloodline for her own reasons.

To make a long story short, White Head Daddy gave my grandmother four children: two boys and two girls. After the birth of the fourth child, family members claim that my grandmother got wet in a rainstorm while gathering firewood, became sick, and died. In 1902, my natural mother was the second child born of the relationship between Henry Parker and his young, Irish mistress. Aunt Lela, my mother, and their two brothers were without a mother by 1908, when the games really began.

My grandfather's wife, Flora Parker, had already given him eight children. However, upon the death of his mistress, my maternal grandmother, Flora Parker—playing the dutiful and faithful wife—took the four "bastard" children into her home to raise them as her own. That's when the systematic abuse of these four children commenced behind their father's back while he worked the land. She would beat Lela over the head with words of torture about her mother's adulterous ways and how Lela was conceived in sin.

Flora Parker, or Aunt Flo as Lela called her, had tall stature and such fair skin as to be able to "pass" for white. She also had that "good hair" that was so prized in those days. Day upon unmerciful day, Aunt Flo low-rated, degraded, and beat Lela and her siblings—forcing them to eat their food from granite dishes while sitting on the floor drinking Blue John Milk (milk that was blue tinged and came from cows that ate bitterweed). Meanwhile, her eight children sat at a table for meals with proper linen and silverware.

For unknown reasons, possibly because she was the eldest of the four, Aunt Lela felt so torn between her father's children, *the eight*, and her mother's children, *the four*. Her father's children were considered better than her mother's children. The four were considered bastards. And *the eight* grew up making sure the other four children knew their place. Yet, Lela idolized her stepmother and her siblings and even tried to emulate the oldest of them.

She also adored her father. She described in detail every hill, field, horse, cow, cotton-ball, and blade of grass. She recalled the little house where her mother and father had begotten *the four*—right on her daddy's property. Lela always spoke with such pride in her voice about being Henry Parker's daughter. He had given her a gift once—a horse— and Lela seemed to grow taller in stature when she spoke of that horse—a beloved gift from her dad. Somehow, I feel Lela knew her father loved her despite all the pain she endured because of his "sinful" ways.

In my eyes as a child, I felt deeply insulted by *the eight*. I hated them, having just left Heaven. I knew their hearts and their truth. I saw every stuck up nose on their high yellow faces with the long, flowing hair properly done up in buns and braids—and it all centered on my mother. Over the course of my mother's life, she married several times while all the sisters of the eight died having the same husband. My birth mother was Henry Parker's pride and joy, the pick of the litter, and she didn't give a damn who knew she was daddy's girl. Even though *the eight* talked about my mother, they also held a secret pride in her.

At 16, my mother married a WWI veteran. The day she met him he was driving a surrey with the fringe on the top—a big deal back in those times. Then, on the day of her wedding, she finally broke down and told White Head Daddy about all the bad and evil things that had been done behind his back to *the four* during their childhood. She spoke of having to eat on granite plates on the floor like dogs while *the eight* sat at the table proper. She lamented about the back breaking work, the bitter, ugly words against their mother they had to endure, and the beatings laid to their backs at the hands of their stepmother. Lela said her father cried like a baby upon hearing all this. *The four* were so happy my mother had finally let it all out. White Head Daddy begged their forgiveness for all that had been done to them and life was much better afterwards.

Living under all this, I often wondered how Aunt Lela

managed to keep it together at all. A doctor once told me she had quiet hysteria and that she was abusive towards me due to mental illness. In today's society they would diagnose her with bipolar disorder.

I remember one day, coming home from school and being asked by Lela to bury a can of saltpeter (Potassium nitrate used in explosives and fertilizer,

and as a food additive, once believed to have the power to stop an erection, also used in making magic potions) under the steps. When I asked her for a reason, she became hysterical. I did it anyway but somehow, I just knew it was something weird. Was its witchcraft?

Then there were the times Aunt Lela woke me early

in the morning and sent me to Ann Bank's Street to steal gravel and rocks for her flower beds and plants. She really did have a green thumb! Everything she planted grew and prospered. I remember the specific morning, she woke me to announce we we're planting oak trees. We lived in a cul-de-sac in the center of the street. She had me dig three large holes, pour in water, shovel the saplings into the holes and then refill the holes with earth to cover the saplings. I firmly packed the dirt around them and when we were finished, she hauled off and slapped me across the face then strolled into the house. It's many years later, yet every time I go home and see those trees I cry.

Many nights I went to bed so wounded from her words: Aunt Lela was never silent. She continuously brow beat me about my mother.

BRUDDER FALL ME DOWN

"She's no good," Lela would say, "marrying all those men; she's just a whore and a ne'er-do-well, and you will be just like her".

Oftentimes, after a beating, which included Lela calling me a "bastard" and telling me that I wasn't as good as the other girls in the neighborhood, I would cut across the local graveyard and finally release the tears. This began my lifetime of crying to keep from dying. Other times I would go outside to sit with my dog, Blacky, and the cat, Molly.

"I know my mother loves me!" I would cry out to God. I sat expressing my pain and the animals would snuggle close to me, warm and sweet, as if they understood me. Sometimes the three of us fall fast asleep under the mimosa tree.

I have often wondered if Lela ever realized she treated me the exact way her stepmother had treated *the four*. But I still feel good when I think of Lela's good days. She would wake me early—as you can see, everything with this woman was "early to bed and early to rise"— and she would make hot biscuits. She opened jars of preserves: mine was pears, hers was figs. She would prepare a pot of coffee and talk, talk, talk! Always she wanted to talk about Aunt Flo and her father Henry Parker. She discussed the "good times"; the picnics and church socials at Mount Charity Missionary Baptist Church. That church is over 150 years old and my entire family is recorded there. Even me! Lela said they wear white lawn dresses and pongee gowns.

I would sit listening and visualizing her—tall, young, beautiful, and strong.

Chapter II

Miss Alabama Mary

I cannot remember a time when I wasn't reading. Some family members say that I have read an entire library. I do know it is very hard for me to breathe without a book somewhere near me. I learned to read very young in my life; long before I became of age for school.

An old lady lived in our neighborhood whom I will never forget. She wore shabby clothing and candy-apple red lipstick all over her face. She was not a clown in my eyes, although the other residents of the neighborhood seemed to be afraid of her and laughed behind her back. Her house sat alone on the block facing the railroad tracks. Folks called it haunted. She had so much clutter in her yard and on the walls of her house that people referred to her as the "Hoo-Doo Lady" or "Miss Alabama Mary".

My sister and the other kids in the neighborhood feared approaching her but for some unknown reason I did not. I adored her! I started our friendship by simply saying "howdy-doo" to her whenever I saw her.

One year, while I lived with my birth mother (my Aunt sent me to live with my birth mother once a year until I was a teenager), I had the opportunity to visit with Miss Alabama Mary. She had so much to see at her house in all that clutter. She had stacks and stacks of magazines in her home and didn't mind my looking through them. *Life, The New Yorker, National Geographic, Sepia, Modern Romance,* and many others; it was a heaven of words to me! There were newspapers too: *The Pittsburgh Courier, The Chicago Defender* and *The Clarion Ledger.* I learned to read by looking through those magazines and newspapers. Miss Alabama Mary would tell me the words I didn't know and what they meant. I spent hours in her haunted, lonely house just reading, reading, reading!

When the circus came to town that year, we had the customary big parade as always and my birth mother allowed us to go. That was the difference between my mother and her sister. When living with my mother, we could explore life, we had a sense of well-being, and we had adventures.

The parade began a block from Aunt Lela's house
and continued through town to the fairgrounds
down "under the hill". Miss Alabama Mary started
marching with the elephants, lions, and all the other
animals they had in the parade! With my natural flair
for adventure, I joined the procession with Miss
Alabama Mary and also began the march to the
fairgrounds.

I could feel the power of the drums beating in my
heart. Though the animals smelled, the lions and
elephants looked regal and majestic in their walk.
And the clowns were, well, clowning. I got so swept
up in the magic of it all, I even wished I could wear
candy-apple red lipstick just like Miss Alabama Mary.

Suddenly, I was snatched out of one of the most

beautiful moments in my life by my Aunt Lela. It was time for me to go back home and I never got to march in another parade again.

Chapter III
Miss Mississippi

I did not start out my life thinking I was pretty or even cute. In fact, growing up, the old folks never called me pretty. But Aunt Lela always told my older sister Sua how beautiful she was. That hurt me so much because we differed in our skin color. Sua was a smooth black and I was yellow. On those days, when Lela was in her divide and conquer mode, she praised my sister and totally ignored me. Then, she would comment on how silky Sua's hair was.

"The blacker the berry the sweeter the juice," she would say. This talk would almost kill me, but I never said a word because I loved my Sua and I wanted her to feel pretty. I never let on that I had these feelings about Lela making a difference between the two of us. I just suffered in silence and dreamed of growing up and becoming Miss

Mississippi.

My sister did little things like stealing and lying then expected me to cover for her. I forever felt nervous and scared because I never knew what kind of trouble Sua would get us into next. In the hallway sat a telephone table where my grandmother kept a quarter under a scarf on the table. The quarter had been there so long it left an imprint. One day Sua decided to take the quarter. When Lela discovered that the infamous quarter was missing, my sister, looking all silky hair and "blacker the berry" looked my grandmother dead in her eyes and said I took it! I cannot describe the sense of shock and betrayal to my nine-year-old mind and heart but I can describe the pain my body felt from the leather strap. Lela punished me, though I'd done no wrong. That day the thought of suicide first took root in my young, fertile mind. I started to sit beneath the mimosa tree and beg God to let me die!

Unlike Sua, I was mostly praised for pleasing people.
When Aunt Lela expressed her pleasure and
appreciation for all I'd done for her, it made me so
happy. And at that time it was all I had to hold on to.
So, I would run around trying to please everyone in
the house, the neighborhood, the world. Whew!
You can imagine how traumatic it was then when
Aunt Lela, after having a conversation with my sister,
came into the house screaming and beating me for
being bad. When that beating ended, I took over a
hundred aspirin and proceeded to pound my head
repeatedly against a steel post. I first attempted
suicide at the ripe old age of 11.

I had a hard time within myself after that; a hard time
with self-confidence and controlling my thoughts.
On the surface I'm sure I appeared to be a normal
11-year-old, but I was already severely bruised and
battered mentally as well as physically. Let me tell

you, Satan came in and twisted the situation, making me a very compulsively manic individual. The cycle of abuse that had begun with Aunt Flo and the four continued in me.

My family either did not notice the changes in me or decided to ignore them as many will choose to do. When my sister married at the age of 12, I felt devastated. But I must admit things did get a little better for me with Lela. When things were not good, I, in turn, immersed myself in books and work.

I was educated at a private white faculty Catholic school and then graduated from one of the oldest public schools in Jackson, Mississippi. And I got a job working in the biggest cafeteria in the city. In those years you could work in a grown person's place; you just walked into the boss' office, introduced yourself, and told him you were the replacement. For obvious reasons, I felt happiest when at school or work. I also very actively participated in church and civic activities. Throughout my childhood, people often referred to me as "the busiest little girl in town". Even Lela spoke of how smart I was. I so much wanted to go on to college and I dreamed of being a missionary. From a very young age I knew I wanted to be in service to the Lord.

You must understand I had no way of knowing what was best for me at that time in my life. I raised myself to the best of my ability. I say I raised myself because after a while Aunt Lela became so sickly that I had to take care of everything. This included all the business of running the household. I could "homestead" a piece of property with the best of the grown-ups. I could prepare a meal for a party of twenty as well as for the immediate family. Whatever it took to make my Aunt Lela happy I did…and more. Now, looking back over my life, I can clearly see and comprehend what was happening in my mind. I, having no one to really talk to and share my dreams with, spent the majority of my time trying to please others. I felt pitifully sad and lonely. But no one could take from me my nightly talks with God. I would tell Him of all my troubles. From the age of 9 to 19, I would sit under the mimosa tree and cry out to Him. On other nights, I would be so filled with His spirit and joy that I would sing into the night with the lightning bugs flitting around as my only audience. At the age of 15, a neighbor dying with cancer gave me the greatest compliment I've ever received. He told me about my singing under the mimosa tree on those lonely, silence-filled nights eased his pain and made it possible for him to sleep. That is a moment I will never forget.

***

As I've said before, I am a product of my

environment, as are all persons, but growing up in the segregated South made it very frustrating to be young, gifted, and black. I have danced and acted on stages throughout my life, but at that time, there were no schools of dance or acting in my hometown. So, I went to the library and read books on the art of ballet and modern dance. I'd then take what I learned back to school and teach these steps to our dance class. I also acted in drama clubs and in small theaters throughout the city. I felt blessed to have some of the most dedicated teachers one could ever want. When they saw my talents in the arts they did all they could to help me. This was kind of unique in the South at that time.

When I was planning my wedding, my Home Economics teacher actually came to my home to offer her assistance and brought two others teacher with her. Together they planned the

most beautiful wedding for me; it was the talk of
our town.

The year I graduated from high school turned out
to be both happy and tragic. I got married and
went on to enroll in one of the finest private
Christian colleges in the South. But my Aunt Lela
husband Guy Hopkins, who had ironically become
my best-friend, died from cancer that very same
year.

Eventually, I became Miss Mississippi—
participant in fashion shows, beauty contests, and
talent contests throughout the state. By the grace
of God, I didn't manage to kill myself and I grew up.

Chapter IV
Talking with God & the NAACP

This morning I lay half-awake, half-asleep thinking about my life—about all the talks from the heart I've had with God. I reflected on the times spent sitting under the Mimosa tree talking and sharing with Him. Whatever the trouble of the day, I would strain to hold back the tears and sorrow until my housework and homework was done, and I could go outside; until the time came to have my talk with God under my tree. I know those talks are the reason I am alive today to talk with you.

Initially I wanted this book to be a tool for young girls and boys who feel like the underdogs. As years advanced, the book transformed into a how-to manual on screwing up your life without realizing it. However, now that I see and read so much about young people who desire to take life and to commit suicide, I feel it is my duty to tell my story. I pray it will help the young and restless with their lack of respect for life.

Another reason I wrote this book is to ask children to just talk to God. He is able to hear you. I want you to know that no matter what you may go through in life, God will make it possible for you to find your way. No matter what happened or didn't happen, good or bad, I always talked to God about it. I talked to Him before, during and after it happened; I never stopped talking to God. Somehow, even as a child, I knew in my DNA that I had to talk to God.

As I grew older and got married, I could see life more clearly. I began to understand how people operated with me and how others viewed me. People saw me as someone to use and then laugh at—the one you called on only when you needed something.

I vividly remember one of the most awesome times in my life. I belonged to and worked for one of this country's most powerful organizations: The National Association for the Advancement of Colored People (NAACP). On one particular day, we instigated a boycott against several businesses in the area. Fellow members of the organization chose me to act as a spy during this boycott.

Now at that time, there were only two streets in my town for commerce—one for white-owned businesses and one for black-owned. My assignment was to walk alone down the white street to verify that no blacks were patronizing the white-owned businesses. As I began my assignment, I had no fear. But then I noticed how eerie, silent, long, and bleak Capitol Street was and it kind of worked on my nerves. To me it seemed as if there was not a man or woman of color on Earth that day. Not even one in the whole of the Universe. I could feel the hair crawling up the back of my neck and my legs wanted to wobble, but I would not allow that. I could see the faces peering out at me from behind the empty shop windows, but no one said a word. I knew I had to walk tall, proud, and not show any signs of fear.

When I returned to the command post to give my report on shaky legs, everyone was happy and excited that the boycott was a success. Then, the most awful thing happened. While they all congratulated each other, I suddenly noticed everyone pointing and laughing in my direction. I had assumed they would be proud and pleased with my actions until I realized they were laughing at me—not with me. They commented on how I was the only one crazy enough to go out there and test the situation. These people had indeed risked my life and now made me the butt of their joke. Let me say it was in no way funny to me. I felt crushed to say the least.

I pray I never hurt anyone the way my colleagues hurt me. Again, I talked to God and spilled out my pain to him.

As I moved on in life, I traveled to many places and saw many new and different faces, soon forgetting my days in the Civil Rights Movement; however, I can give a first-hand account of those times and the contribution I made no matter how great or small. I do still miss those that have gone on before me as I continued to walk, talking with God.

Chapter V
Sister

My life really didn't begin until I arrived in Los Angeles, California. I woke early one morning in Jackson, Mississippi assessing my life, my marriage, and my motherhood. Yes, by this time I had a child. I decided right then my child would not grow up in a separate but unequal environment. So, I formed a plan of escape with California as my destination. After my husband left for work, I gave everything we owned to his mother and the neighbors. The day we moved, he came home to an echo!

Mr. Pedro, our next-door neighbor growing up, first spoke of the beauty of California. I shined his shoes for him and listened to him repeatedly describe it as a paradise. He had been to so many places like

Florida and Havana, Cuba working as a migrant fruit picker; but, California was his favorite of all places. Through his words I could see the colorful trees and flowers, the white beaches, and the startling blue skies in my mind's eye. I could smell the air on the ocean breezes. I could feel the warmth of the sun's rays. His descriptive words had ignited the flame of desire in me. I was excited to get to California in a hurry.

On the corner of Sunset and Vine, the most famous corner in the world, I saw mud. Mud in paradise! Mud in California! For some reason I cried. Of course, after that bit of culture shock I immediately became a "California Nut without a Shell"!

***

Not long after arriving in Los Angeles, I found her: my sweet sister Sua. Sua had married at the age of 12 to a much older man that had abused and battered her monstrously over the years. I had cried and longed to see her because our last meeting had been brought on by violence so horrific that I still can't look at any man without seeing it. Sua and I had to bury her baby boy because Sua's twisted husband had literally beaten the baby out of her while I stood watching—paralyzed and helpless with fear (I really had to talk to God about that one!).

They arrested Sua's husband, thank God, and he served his time at the Governor's Mansion. He was what they called a "trustee" and would be out on the mansion lawn working on the landscaping. I would ride by and taunt him every day.

"What bird can't fly?" I would scream in his direction. He couldn't answer me because they forbade the trustees to speak to anyone except his superiors and other inmates. He couldn't answer but he could and would hear me. This served me well! I would continue the taunt by answering my own question.

"A JAIL BIRD!" I would scream again—this time at the top of my lungs.

Shortly afterward, they released him. Then, he stole out of town on the sneak with my sister and their three-year-old daughter.

When I finally found her, she came running along the side of her house with seven little ones behind her. She weighed over 200 pounds and her teeth were all either broken or missing. Her face and arms did not have a smooth, unscarred piece of flesh left on them; they were covered in knife wounds. And her house was nothing but a pigsty set behind a larger house. Believe me, I wanted to die when I saw all this.

I felt so sad for her, having to be married to this evil man, who battered, beat, and kept her "barefoot and pregnant" all the time. By the age of 24, she was already the mother of 12 children—5 of whom were stillborn because of the beatings Sua's husband laid upon her during the early stages of her pregnancies. At that moment I hated him and all the hims of the world.

Needless to say, I had my work cut out for me with my sister. We were able to get rid of my sister's abusive husband by having him arrested again. This time, I walked in and found him struggling with her to take her $119 check. I ran across the room striking him with my fist. He hit me then slammed me into the screen door. The door came off the hinges with me on top of it. Someone called the police. When we made it to court, they sentenced him to three years and my sister was finally free! She then applied for a divorce, receiving it speedily because he was a known batterer of women—me included.

I had learned from neighbors and other sources the true extent of the abuse Sua had suffered at his hands. Not only did he beat her, but he took to throwing knives at and into her body from across the room. She would try to run from him and escape the violence but to no avail. I heard tales of the blood loss and the bloody handprints on the walls each time he cut her.

On several occasions when the ambulance arrived at the hospital, the staff had placed toe tags on her toe and a red blanket over her because she was presumed dead on arrival. Then, by the grace of God, a finger or toe would twitch, and they would revive her. My sister would live another day to tell her story. The entire sordid business left a bitter taste in my mouth and I never wanted to marry another man after that.

With Sua's husband gone, I got busy cleaning up our lives. I found a huge house that would accommodate me, my 18-month-old son, my sister, and her seven children. I was so very happy for my child. He could grow up surrounded by "brothers and sisters"— something I had missed out on while growing up. In those early California days I felt like my life was coming together for the first time in years. I was really happy about that so, like with all things in my life, I shared this with God.

Chapter VI

Mother

I loved Los Angeles. You never had to be without money in this city. You could lie in the sun poolside, sit in the sauna, or relax in the whirlpool carousing through the unemployment section of the *Daily News* for a job. People sold roses on street corners, earned money from building churches, and God knows what else. Oranges made the stock market billions of dollars every year.

I've seen men sell bolts without nuts in service station parking lots and it excited me so much I would be late getting to church. I would actually get out of my car and help them count!

After moving to California, I spent the mid years of

my life here as a wife, mother, and businesswoman.
I became the first black go-go girl in Los Angeles in
the early '60s. Go-go girls helped promote the local
events and nightclubs.

From there, I also played a role in breaking the color
barrier in the motion picture industry working as a
hairdresser, make-up artist, and freelancer for
some of the biggest stars of that time. Not only did
I work with all the major studios, but my travels have
taken me to many states and countries.

I did well enough to own a salon and wig shop.
Eventually, I incorporated both a modeling agency
and a clothing boutique into the original business.
The modeling agency would go on to produce
fashion shows at several ritzy eating establishments
around the city.

***

California had been good to me, and I was flying pretty high. So after much thought and many sessions with my new psychiatrist, I decided to face the biggest demon in my life: my bastard-ship.

My mother lived in Northern California with two of my older sisters. I hopped a plane and went to see her to face my past. It hurt me so bad to see how my mother was living. She resided in a basement apartment that belonged to one of her church members. I asked her to come to Southern California to live with me instead. I packed all her belongings and sent them ahead and we flew back to L.A. together.

When we arrived, I surprised her with the cutest little one bedroom sporting its own backyard. She even ended up getting a little dog named Daisy.

One day I mustered up enough nerve to ask her why she had given me up. Yeah, that took some courage! She answered that I was special and that her sister could take much better care of me than she could at the time. Really? Let me tell you, I wanted to slap that silly woman's face but of course I didn't. After all she was my mother, and we were together at last. I was determined to give my mother the best possible life.

By the time I had been in Los Angeles for a couple of years, I was making big moves. I worked the salon and produced fashion shows at three or four nightclubs in the city during their businessmen luncheons. I took Mother everywhere I went, introduced her to every celebrity I knew, and bought her a wardrobe to die for. Pleasing Mother became my new obsession.

My mother even worked as one of the models in my shows. She was still a beautiful woman and everyone just loved her! To say that I was happy to have her in my life is an understatement; I was ecstatic. My son also adored her. They worshipped each other.

***

In my short life, I had

never met anyone who worshipped God more than my mother did back then. She prayed every day, all day. I would come home from work and hear my mother praying for someone over the telephone.

"That's alright, honey. God will fix it!" She

replied no matter what folks said to her about the troubles of life and the problems of the world.

Or "I've got Jesus and that's enough." She would thank Him for everything.

I clearly remember the excitement I would feel for winning awards and receiving honors for my civic and community work. I would rush home to share it with my mother.

Mother would look at me and say "Ledora, you need Jesus". It was as simple as that. At least until her health began to fade.
I noticed her eyesight wasn't great, so I took her to see a top eye-laser surgeon.

He recommended operating. She had two eyes surgeries: one in May of that year and then another in December. Thankfully the surgeons helped restore her eyesight and crowned her belle of the hospital. A soft, gentle woman and the quintessential "Southern belle", people were just crazy about my mother! I walked into her hospital room once to find her eating peppermint candy with one of the famous actors in the world. The two of them were throwing the candy wrappers on the floor and laughing like two children. They shared the same doctor and were having the same type of surgery. I look back now and thank God, He allowed me to give my mother some fun and happiness in her lifetime.

Not too long afterward, a neighbor reached out to tell me that my mother would sweep the floors all day and night. When I went to check on her, she got up and immediately began sweeping. I looked around and noticed her house wasn't as neat and tidy as she usually kept it. I packed her up and moved her in with us thinking maybe she just felt lonely. She did seem to cheer up a bit, at first, but the situation turned for the worse.

I started receiving calls at work informing me that my mother was wandering alone down the street. I would rush home at once. We took her too the doctor and the diagnosis weren't good. They informed us our mother was in the first stages of Alzheimer's disease. This devastated me! The physicians advised me to place her in a convalescent home.

"No, never!" I shouted. I could and would never do that to her. I kept her at home and hired help.

Never in my life have I ever witnessed such an illness as Alzheimer's. I watched my mother slowly forget the most important and special people in her life: her children. I look back now and thank God He allowed me to give my mother some fun and happiness in her lifetime.

Chapter VII

The Fashion Show

I had a dream one night about a sit-down dinner in a fashion show setting. I saw well-dressed individuals admiring stunning models as they paraded down the runway. When I awoke, I knew this was a once in a lifetime vision for me!

The very next day a very important member of the film industry had an appointment with me for a haircut. A mutual friend and father-figure to us both had introduced us. Well, during our appointment, I spoke of my dream and my desire to perform it on the stage of a very prestigious hotel in the city. He responded that he'd lend his name to my project and work for me for scale. If I earned more than a specific amount, we both agreed that I would pay him more. We sealed the deal with a handshake. *What was I thinking?* I thought to myself. I had to be crazy to think I could pull this off!

Well, as the old saying goes, all hell broke loose. My friend went to jail for tax evasion on the same day my tickets went on sale.

I was up to my neck in work with models to train, dancers to teach, and musicians to hire. Then I had to ensure my vision came through to the designers, hair stylists, and make-up artists. People, questions, and decisions were everywhere. Among them, of course, were the naysayers reminding me that I couldn't pull this off. Although they hurt me the most, I had so many clients who came to my rescue! So many were willing to step in and offer a helping hand, that even to this day it warms my heart. It feels good to remember how they banded together with the public to make my dream a reality. We would work all day and then stay up all night—gluing feathers on coats *exactly* like I had seen in my night vision!

Considering I was the producer, director, and coordinator for this project, I worked 24 hours a day around the clock. I would pull strangers off the street to come sit with me while I designed and sewed the garments I had envisioned. One month into my work on the project, I even helped get my friend out of jail. We had experienced the miracle of a lifetime.

Every major television and media station made an appearance when my friend got released. I saw this as a good opportunity to advertise and promote my production. Ticket sales blew up and went through the roof!

But if I learned anything from this endeavor, my fifteen minutes of fame taught me you can't trust anyone. I have never seen people act the way they acted the day of production. People displayed envy, jealousy, and yes, even hate towards me. People were even calling me names. I had mixed emotions because I couldn't understand how I generated such a crown.

My knees shook for a lot of the occasion, so it took my friend and a security guard to hold me up. In the end, though, it all worked out just fine. We had a successful production and we got good reviews! I will forever remember the faithfulness of those that stuck with me—those that had my back when I needed it the most.

Chapter VIII

Brudder Fall Me Down

I was 23 years old when the nightmare first began. My friend Brudder[1] and I were having dinner with two other friends at a beautiful 5-star restaurant. As the waiters served us cognac, Brudder pulled a thousand-dollar bill from his wallet and proceeded to roll it between his thumb and index fingers. He took a sip of his cognac, placed the rolled-up bill to his nose, and sniffed some white powder from a small mirror on the table. Our two companions followed suit. I sat watching in stunned silence. Brudder then offered me a sniff.

"What is this?" I asked.

"The sport of kings and queens," he responded.

Never having heard the word "cocaine" before in my life, I trusted him. I trusted Brudder completely. He taught me how to snort it properly right there at the table. Yes, right there in that fancy 5-star restaurant.

I had never felt that good in my entire life. Suddenly the environment became magical; the silver shone brighter while the atmosphere and my surroundings took on a whole new opulence. It felt like I was...home.

When I returned to my actual house, I had an overpowering urge to feel water on my skin. I disappeared in the shower. When I had re-emerged, six hours had passed. Yes, you read it correctly; I stayed in that shower for a whole six hours! From that moment on, water played a huge part in my use of cocaine. It seemed to revive me and make me feel alive.

It wasn't long before I found out several of my girlfriends and female clients were also using it. Soon I connected with a dealer that gladly delivered.

I lived and worked in L.A. in the times of hippies and Woodstock. But it was also a time of war and death. Someone had just murdered the President as the Vietnam War worried me and the entire nation. Folks tried very hard to love one another and bring peace to a chaotic world. We often felt free on one hand and sad on the other.

In my personal life, I was in the middle of a divorce and a newly single mother. I lost family and friends left and right. These were very uncertain times and I felt scared to death of many things.

Without really thinking about it, I jumped right on the cocaine bandwagon with my friend. It seemed a "toot" could fix just about anything. My favorite form of relaxation included doing a line of coke while sitting in the tub or Jacuzzi. I would just sit there and think about life.

I worked two jobs and attended beauty school. One of those jobs involved dancing as a "go-go girl" and I must admit I did that very well. I was the first black go-go dancer in my area. As the sole person responsible for taking care of a child and a home, holding down two to three jobs while going to school wore me out. But I made it. Around the same time that I started cocaine I also found my Sua and reunited with my mother. A lot went on in my life, but they never knew about my addiction. I just got that good at keeping my secret.

Eventually I finished beauty school and opened my first beauty business. Soon, it was the talk of the town! In the '70s, the money kept circulating and business could not have been better for me.

The nature of my business, working in the Motion

Picture Industry (MPI), kept me hobnobbing with the jetsetters of the times. I have never felt better than when I received my first paycheck and saw the deduction for the retirement home of the MPI. I also felt privileged to have been part of breaking the color barriers in film. I truly was on my way!

I dated what was called a "high-roller" in those days. Sometimes my friends and I would leave the shop in our work clothes, hop a plane, change while on the plane, and then step off the plane dressed to the nines for a night of gambling and shows. All of this felt very exciting for a young woman from Mississippi. We were having a ball—or at least we thought we were.

***

Everybody who was somebody wanted me to do their hair. I had clients that would fly in from New York or Paris at all hours of the day or night, whenever they finished a job or business deal. I stayed ready to accommodate them. With the help of cocaine, I soon learned I could stay awake working for 12 or 15 hours straight every day never closing shop. I had even begun to smoke cigarettes because my nose would swell and turn red from the cocaine use. It was definitely a warning, but I did not take heed. Instead, I just learned a new way to intake the drug—through the end of a cigarette filter.

Whenever I saw a star "burnout" or heard of someone getting arrested for using, I experienced a moment of clarity and would stop. Sometimes I stopped for as long as a year. But the demon depression would always come-a-calling then, I would start up again.

You see I was not spiritually aware at that time. I searched for the answers to life probably harder

BRUDDER FALL ME DOWN

than I partied. Whenever people invited me to their church or cult I would go. But I couldn't find my idea of truth. The fear in my heart had me hating God. I especially bound by fear when hearing the words "thy" and "thou" in the Bible. Near my salon sat a huge parking lot. In the deep of night, I would sit out there shouting.

"Where are you, God? If you are God, show yourself to me!"

I grew up in a home full of abuse while my Aunt force fed me guilt for the sins of others. I had seen plenty of the devil in people, but I was not sure about God anymore. Gone was the faith of that little girl who sat beneath the Mimosa tree and talked to God. That girl knew God was there and listened. She had been replaced by someone who feared and felt burned out by the hurts and wrongs of life at the hands of the people she loved and trusted the most. I even decided not to attend church anymore. I remember witnessing two women fighting over the Pastor while he steadily watched me one Sunday. How ironic. They were trying to kill each other over him and he couldn't take his eyes off me.

In 1974, I began taking dying seriously again. I could only think of the pain I had endured throughout my life, the nightmares, and the mental and physical abuse. Constantly, I wondered how to make it through life as a single woman and mother with all the things that go bump in the night.

Chapter IX

Big Poppa

At the height of my professional success, I became acquainted with a very well-respected and wise man. All my friends flocked to his home once or twice a week to swim in his pool or sit in his sauna. We would sit at his feet like he was Jesus, listening to him expound on his life in *the life*. He had been everywhere and seen everything. Not to mention he served up cocaine like it was legal and we all ate it up.

He treated me like a little sister. He even seemed to watch out for me. He and I would have long talks deep into the night so I learned a lot of wisdom about life and how to deal with people from this man. I spent the majority of my spare time at his home because I felt very alone at this point in my life. I dealt with all kinds of thought patterns at that time. I wasn't sleeping well and believed I heard voices. The voices loved to tell me that I hadn't created much in life. They said I was nothing and that I would always be nothing more than a bastard. To survive, I sat up talking all night and worked all day. When it got to be too much, I would call Big Poppa and he would tell me to come over. We'd do a line or two, and I would relax and let my guard down. Then and only then, could I speak of my childhood or other parts of my life. I felt I could not discuss that with anyone else.

In response, Big Poppa often told me to settle down. He believed that I tried too hard to please people and to live too perfectly. He explained that all that fear I had in me wasn't doing me any good at all. Big Poppa suggested I stop living my life for others because when I really needed them, they would not be there for me. So why should I concern myself with what these very people had to say about me or how have they felt about me? For reasons unknown, I felt I could trust him.

He laughed at everything yet somehow, I knew he wasn't laughing at me. He would laugh at situations I found myself in. Back then I was so naïve I actually believed people who committed crimes for a living didn't celebrate holidays like everyone else. If I showed signs of shock when learning new perspectives about people, he would laugh at my surprise!

Truth be told, every time I ever saw Big Poppa, he was laughing. It was truly a joy just to be around him and I wasn't the only one that felt this way. Folks would come from near and far just to share with him their plans, dreams, and needs. There would be young, old, famous, and everyday people all socializing and uniting at his house.

other night a friend and I discussed how people
who have wealth and fame don't fraternize with
those who don't. That conversation recalled those
days and nights at Big Poppa's house. If I learned one
thing dealing with drugs, it is this: there are no social
boundaries in that world. I know for a fact that
people of all classes and socio-economic situations
gather and deal on the same level when it comes to
drugs. I remember another very famous friend I met
at Big Poppa's home. This individual was a giant in
the business! Yet, I have watched him sit and use
cocaine with a house full of people as if they were
all just eating dinner.

My struggle with cocaine while working in the film
industry also exposed me to many dark and difficult
things. For many years I believed the things I saw
were so awful that I couldn't deal with them at all. I
was still conservative and square in those days—

despite my drug use. On this one night, I was visiting with some high rollers when someone invited us to the alley at the back of the house. At each end of the alley stood a naked girl—I say "girl" because each one looked just out of her teens, if that. These girls were part of a game. The game went like this: on a signal each girl ran from her opposite end to the middle of the alley, where they laid a rock of cocaine about the size of an egg. Whoever got to the middle first had to drop to her knees and pick up the rock with only her mouth. While in this bent position, a man would sodomize each girl. The girl that could pick up the rock while getting sodomized won! Witnessing this, something suddenly came over me. I could not handle it, nor would I stand for it. I commenced yelling and demanded the sick game end! It did. But I was never invited to one of those parties again.

Now the "puff and scratch" parties I could handle. I

loved these the most, so they were the only kind of parties I threw. For a "puff and scratch" event the host had to go to the liquor store, purchase a bottle of champagne, a hundred dollars in lottery tickets, and some rocks, then invite a bunch of friends over. First, you took a "puff" then you would "scratch" off a lottery ticket. Whatever amount you won on the ticket was how many times you had to puff. Imagine what happened to the girl that scratched the hundred-dollar ticket! I never won the game. I was just the nigga spending the money.

Chapter **X**

Base Games

There is so much danger, seen and unseen, in the environment surrounding the use of cocaine. And there was a time not very long ago that under no circumstances could I even speak of this demon. It made me too frightened and ashamed. It has been hard enough to think about it when I am alone with me. Heaven helps me if I thought to share my thoughts with anyone other than those I used with.

In my many years of experience with this drug, it never ceases to amaze me how truly spiritual cocaine is. It can reveal the real character and values of a person in minutes or even seconds. I have watched two people sitting together and suddenly the trust factor just disappears between the two of them. It doesn't matter if it's a husband and wife, sister and brother, or lifelong friends. You could lay a rock down on a table, leave the room, and when you returned either the whole rock or at least part of it had disappeared. The mystery of who took what led to the distrust among users. It's almost as if a spirit of division would come between the two and zap! Just like that the trust and camaraderie in the atmosphere vanishes.

At other times, you had those begging you for it and you refused them at your own peril. I have witnessed very passive people turn very violent behind this stuff.

Then of course there were the moochers—the ones that smile in your face, say all the right words, and as soon as you give them what they want they stop talking to you. This always made me feel bad. Still stuck in my people pleasing phase, I would spend until I had no money left. When I ran out of money, folks would ask me to leave and not come back unless I had something to smoke. If I learned anything good from these "base games" I finally

figured out how to speak my mind after so many years of silence and timidness.

There were also parts of this lifestyle that excited me. Going "on a mission"—when you had to leave home to "cop" or buy drugs—felt like an adventure. The key was to learn to read the signs of the street to avoid danger or getting caught. You had to learn to watch how others walked, talked, and carried themselves to successfully get the products. You did that until you could add your own twist of expertise to the game. If only I had put that much time and effort into perfecting my spiritual and financial growth.

Chapter XI

The Golden Needle

For my own reasons, I have always been a little shy to talk about this but here goes. A friend of mine, who just happened to be a doctor, invited me to a barbeque at their home. Upon arriving, I saw an old girlfriend that I hadn't seen in quite some time. I felt so glad to see her! As she prepared tacos, we talked and at one point she passed me a tile with a line of white on it. I took a toot without a second thought, no doubt. After talking for a few more minutes, I excused myself and walked into the house to greet the host.

About 25 young women seated themselves in the living area—all of them different nationalities and all very beautiful. I remember getting introduced to several of them and walking over to stand by the mantelpiece. The last thing I remember, before blacking out, was standing there in the living area with my elbow on the mantle.

I started to have a dream or a vision. I was in what I call "the Golden Needle". I floated slowly upward. All around me were blond-haired people dressed in all white. I could hear them chanting.

"You are God! You are God!" they said.

I don't know how long it took to travel up that needle but the more I ascended, the more peaceful I felt. The entire time I traveled these angels stayed

with me. I didn't know much about angels then, but I've learned that God has placed them all around us. They constantly ascend and descend reporting to God in Heaven. I feel He placed these angels here just for me.

BRUDDER FALL ME DOWN

When I came back, I saw my taco-\making friend
first. She was crying. Then, the doctor hosting us
grabbed me.

"Welcome back," he stated. But I didn't have
a clue what he meant or why my taco-making friend
was crying until she told me I had died!

The taco-making friend, sometime later, explained
that maybe 30 or 40 minutes after I left her to enter
the house, she came inside. In the living room she
saw me standing stock still at the mantle. She
inquired as to how long I had just been standing
there and someone informed her that I'd been like
that ever since I walked in.

Thank God my host was a doctor! He immediately
began resuscitating me. They worked on me for
hours, from my understanding. They walked me,
slapped me, shook me— everything they could think

of to get me to respond. I remember none of this. I only remember finally coming around and hearing my own voice chanting "I am God". To this very day, this memory of the Golden Needle message frightens me. But it's comforting to know God has His angels all around me.

My legs felt weak, and I didn't feel good at all after waking up. So, my friend decided to take me home with her for a few days. I well remember the car ride to her place.

On the freeway, her car felt more like a spaceship. Everything seemed so intense because the grass was greener, red was redder, and blue was definitely bluer. Things stayed that way for a long time. It took a long while before I felt normal again. That experience taught me to never trust anyone to give me drugs ever again.

Chapter XII

"I Believe Jesus Christ is the Son of God"

There was a period in my life when I truly started living on the edge. I lived with a friend who worked as a con artist. We used heavy duty every day. I had also been using speed. It seems when you try one drug the rest just fall in for whatever reason. I had lost everything including my mind. I even started having awful headaches, stomach cramps, and visions. In the meantime, I ran the streets with my little friend. I could never get the hang of how the con games went, and I didn't have the natural skills to place the cards correctly. So, he elected me to drive for him. Even though I fancied myself in love with him, I hated what he did for a living. But I felt caught up in the whole game and just couldn't let go. One day while circling the block and waiting for him,

I became violently ill. I drove to a girlfriend's house and gave her all my valuables for safekeeping. I asked her to explain my whereabouts to my son and family and then drove myself to the hospital. After the staff checked me in, the doctors explained I was pregnant in my tubes. Somehow, I knew this was my wake up call from God.

I went back to the hospital to have the necessary surgery and while there, I had time to really think about my life and how I had lived it. I felt it best to summarize from the beginning. I came into this

world under extraneous circumstances, was abandoned at birth, and raised in a home where I was not entirely welcomed. I had also lived the major part of my life with bipolar disorder. The phobias I carried with me, whether real or imagined, made me a walking time bomb. My nerves were wrecked. And no matter how brave I pretended to be, I felt terrified of my own shadow.

Upon my release from the hospital, my world as I knew it came crashing down around me. After some thought and debate within myself, I decided to seek professional help. Help arrived in a rather unexpected way.

It was Christmas Eve morning, I will never forget it, and my phone rang.

"Isn't it a joy to celebrate Jesus' birthday?" I answered cheerfully with my holiday greeting. But the young man on the other end only had one question.

"Are you saved, my sister?"
I told him my family had raised me in church but I had become disenfranchised since moving to California and I stopped going. Since I didn't know him, I chose to speak from the heart. I felt a sense

of comfort coming from him through the phone line and all my problems just seemed to roll off my tongue. I confessed my sins to this faceless young man. He then asked if I would accept Jesus Christ as my personal savior. I answered yes. Then, I repeated a prayer after him.

"I believe that Jesus Christ is the Son of God. I believe that He died on the cross for all my sins. Jesus forgives me for all the things I've done wrong! I will serve you in Spirit and in truth from this day forth."

After reciting that prayer, I felt 100 pounds lighter in my spirit! The stranger then proceeded to tell me all about the man I loved and did drugs with. I couldn't remember when I had mentioned anything about him but the stranger knew all about him. He told me how this man had helped plan a city in the southwest and had excelled in high school and college. People highly respected him in the architectural world. This information blew my mind. The telephone stranger told me of a church and its pastor. That pastor taught on faith and since I struggled in that area spiritually, he suggested I study there.

I will never forget this young man and that Christmas Eve morning call. After that moment, I began to rebuild my life. His dialing the wrong number led me to salvation.

It continues to amaze me how God uses all kinds of resources and people to get our attention. I believe He loves us so much; He thinks up all kinds of exciting and new ways to lead us back to Him. It appeared He moved similarly over the lives of many of my friends during this time. Within a short period of time we experienced salvation together just as we had walked the wrong path hand in hand. I can see that has God's love all over that. He knows I'm not the kind of gal that likes to separate from her friends so, He saw fit to bring my friends on the journey with me.

People tell me you will have the same type of personality once saved as you had before salvation. Well, I became quite zealous about witnessing the name of Jesus and what He had done in my life; more so, than I ever was in promoting the party lifestyle.

One of my favorite places to go to witness became this huge park in Los Angeles with a stage where my daughter-in-law and I climb up, sing, and quote Bible passages. In no time people come from all directions and we have a wonderful time sharing the good news.

The best time I ever had in street ministry was when

a traveling minister came to our town to preach.

Afterwards his ministry passed out smiley face stickers. Now he carries a cross on his back as he travels around the world to promote the Gospel of Jesus Christ. When I helped pass out those little stickers it felt so good for my spirit. I walked in high-heels that day and my feet never tired.

Another time, I walked down the street and talked about God with a lady ladling soup out of the trunk of her car. She praised His name for delivering her from addiction and for giving her a home.

It warms my heart to talk to people like this. It helps me get a better look at Jesus and how serving His people free your soul. No, it's not a picnic, but if one wishes to meet God up close and personal ministry is the place for it.

It's wonderful to sit and talk with others who started life walking with God and for whatever reason fell from the faith. It helped me to hear them speak of how unhappy they felt away from Him. That is how I learned to stay prayerful and to stay in the word of God daily so that I would have the backbone to stand up to the adversary when he rears his ugly head.

Black Cloud Over My Head

(A Poem)

Some days I can feel the black cloud following over my head…

I am running under it as fast as I can…

It is speeding up…

I am…

Makes me want to cry out loud…

Stop…Stop…

but I don't because I am around people…

on the job…

in public places…

You see I never knew when the cloud is coming…

I could be doing any number of things…

going about my daily activities…

minding my own business…

and I break out in a cold sweat…

I could hear the voices talking in my head…

voices I had to control…

no matter how so…

I would quickly think or say to myself…

you are going crazy, and the black cloud is going to get you…

don't let it…

I would then reinvent myself to stop the voices and

thoughts…

The method I used to reinvent…

the method would come to me out of the blue…

I would think of someone…

someone I had read about in a book…

I would become that person…

I would change my walk…

my talk…

my hair…

pretend I was another person…

then the black cloud would disappear…

the voices and thoughts would be silenced…

I could sleep and rest…

until the next time…

I've been abandoned by my parents…

denied by my friends…

betrayed by my mind…

I have actually felt like two heads…

two heads growing on my shoulder at one time…

the true head holding a thousand voices…

screaming through my brain…

You are a loser…

You will never make the grade…

bastards don't succeed…

You will never write the book...

You will never be who you are meant to be...

Dear God

(A Poem)

Dear God,

Thank You for staying with me in the years I was
so disconnected from You…

You never left me…

never failed me…

You were there all the time…

Many a day I know I hurt Your heart…

not because I was an evil person…

I didn't have a stony heart…

or not because I was Your enemy…

I was Ignorant…

Ignorant to Your work

Your Word

Your identity

Your promises

And

Ignorant to Your love…

Do You remember the conversations we had from my childhood until today?

Most times I did all the talking…

I was Ignorant to Your ability to speak to me…

Since I couldn't physically hear You…

the enemy took my frustration and caused me to separate from You…

Yes, I know now that there is an enemy…

I just didn't know he was your enemy too…

Yes, I was his tool because I was Ignorant…

Ignorant of his evil

Ignorant of his selfishness

Ignorant of every thought that he has against you…

So, he came to me as an angel of light…

with fun and friendship…

lustful living…

twisting words…

THIS IS THE DAY THAT THE LORD HAS MADE…

I WILL BE GLAD AND REJOICE IN IT…

my Ignorance told me to party on duetted…

So, for forty years me and my Ignorance had the

biggest party…

We wined…

dined…

committed adultery…

gossiped…

drugged…

were puffed up with pride…

scandalized your name…

Now that I am free…

I look back in my spirit…

You were at those parties…

uninvited because of my Ignorance…

yet there because you loved me…

didn't know You existed as I know now…

I'm extending an invitation to another party…

a party of repentance…

a thank You party…

a party of acquaintance…
For I have answered Your invitation when You said
"Behold I stand at the door and knock" …

I say emphatically Yes Lord!

I know from all Your kindness…

Your promises…

Your long-suffering and patience…

You're never leaving me alone…

that this is truly the day that You have made...

and I am peaceful and have joy in it...

Love,

Lucy

under the Mimosa Tree

Epilogue

On November 19, 1996, at 9:00 am, I walked into
Kedren Mental Hospital and committed myself—all
three heads, my dark cloud, and my thousand voices
included.

My life was "tore up from the floor up" as they say
on the street. I spent 72 hours locked in the mental
ward with the mentally insane—me being the
craziest one of them all having been programmed
from birth to believe I was a nobody.

"Girl, you are so crazy!"
"Say something funny for us."
"Why is your eye cocked?"
"Why is your booty so big?"

All the things I heard on a regular basis flooding back
to me. I felt like anyone who was constantly
reminded she was a bastard child with a no good

mother would grow up just like me.

Yet, in that hospital, in the deepest darkest of my pits, I kissed my cocaine addiction goodbye forever.

Made in the USA
Columbia, SC
10 January 2025

50573812R00059